MW00956182

By Dominique Carr

EL'REY SAVES THE DAY

SHARING IS CARING

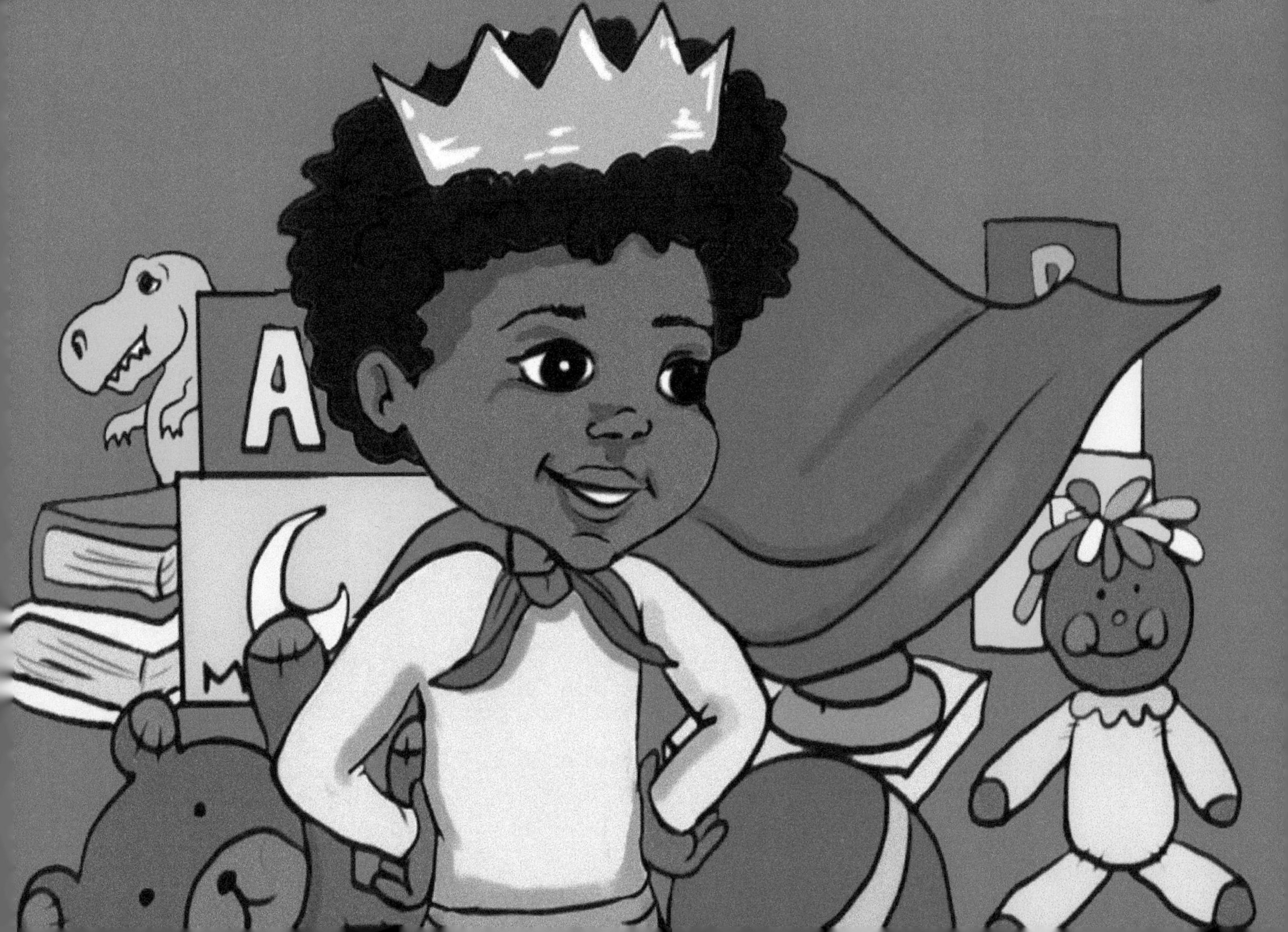
A

Copyright © 2019 Dominique Carr

All rights reserved. No part of this publication may be reproduced, distributed, or transmitted in any form or by any means, including photocopying, recording, or other electronic or mechanical methods, without the prior written permission of the publisher, except in the case of brief quotations embodied in critical reviews and certain other noncommercial uses permitted by copyright law.

ISBN-13: 978-1-970079-43-2

Published by Opportune Independent Publishing Company

For permission requests, write to the publisher, addressed "Attention: Permissions Coordinator" to the address below.

Email: Info@opportunepublishing.com

Address: 113 N. Live Oak Street
Houston, TX 77003

Dedication:

I would like to dedicate this book to El'Rey CARR the inspiration behind the Character El'Rey. It is imperative for our Children to have Role-models and positive representatives that look like them. To all children; you are Royalty! Much love.

One sunny day in the Kindergarten Class. All of the students were cleaning up for recess.

"Okay everyone, it's recess time! Have fun!"
Ms. Jones said excitingly.

KING
ABCDEFG
CAT
123
MATH
SCIENCE
ABC
FAIRYTALES
THREE
PIGS

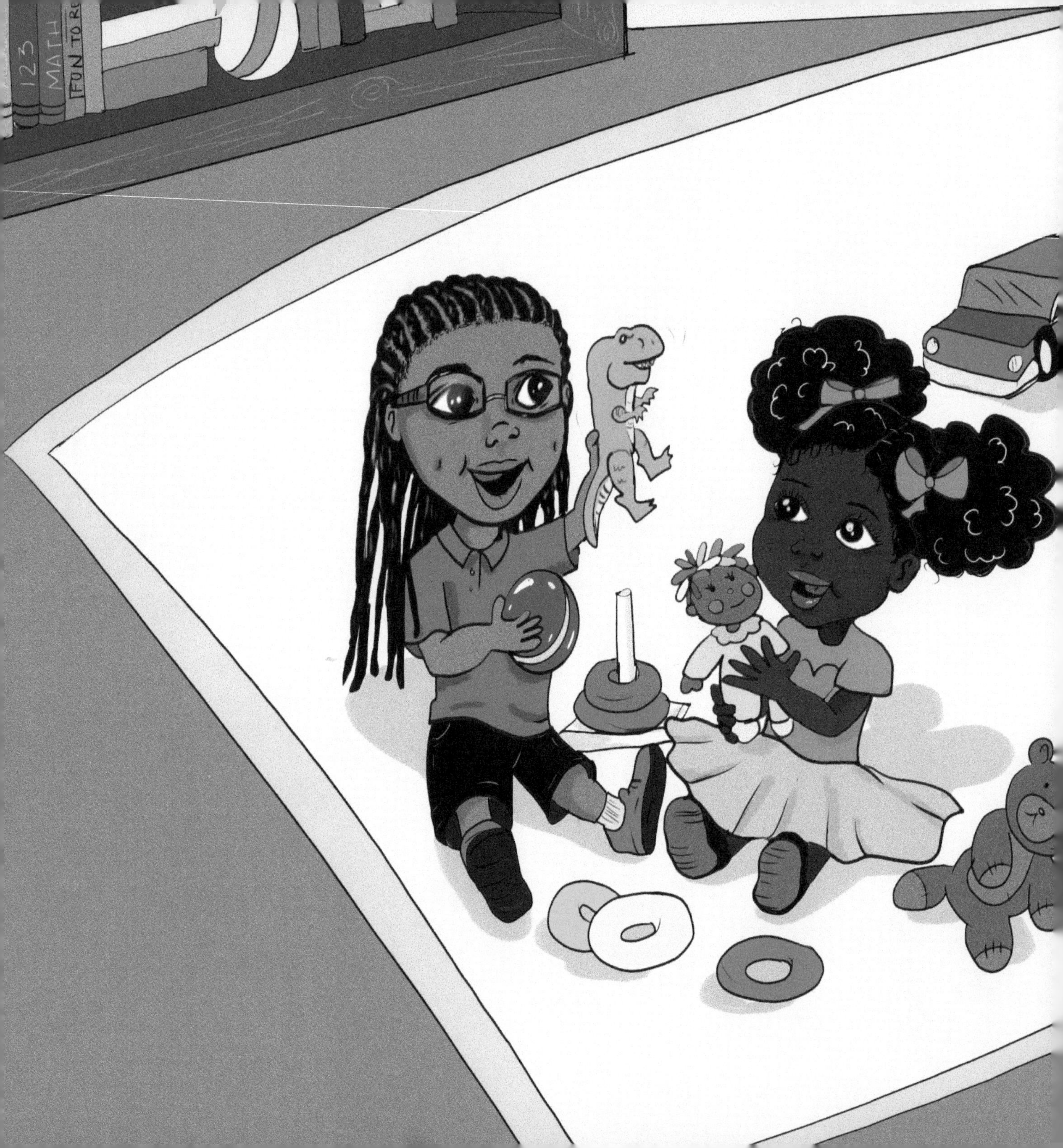
123
MATH

Tasha and Robert went to play with the blocks.

Janaiya walked over and asked Tasha,
"Can I play with your Blocks?"

Tasha replied, "NO! These are Mine!"

"Robert can I play with you?" Janaiya asked.

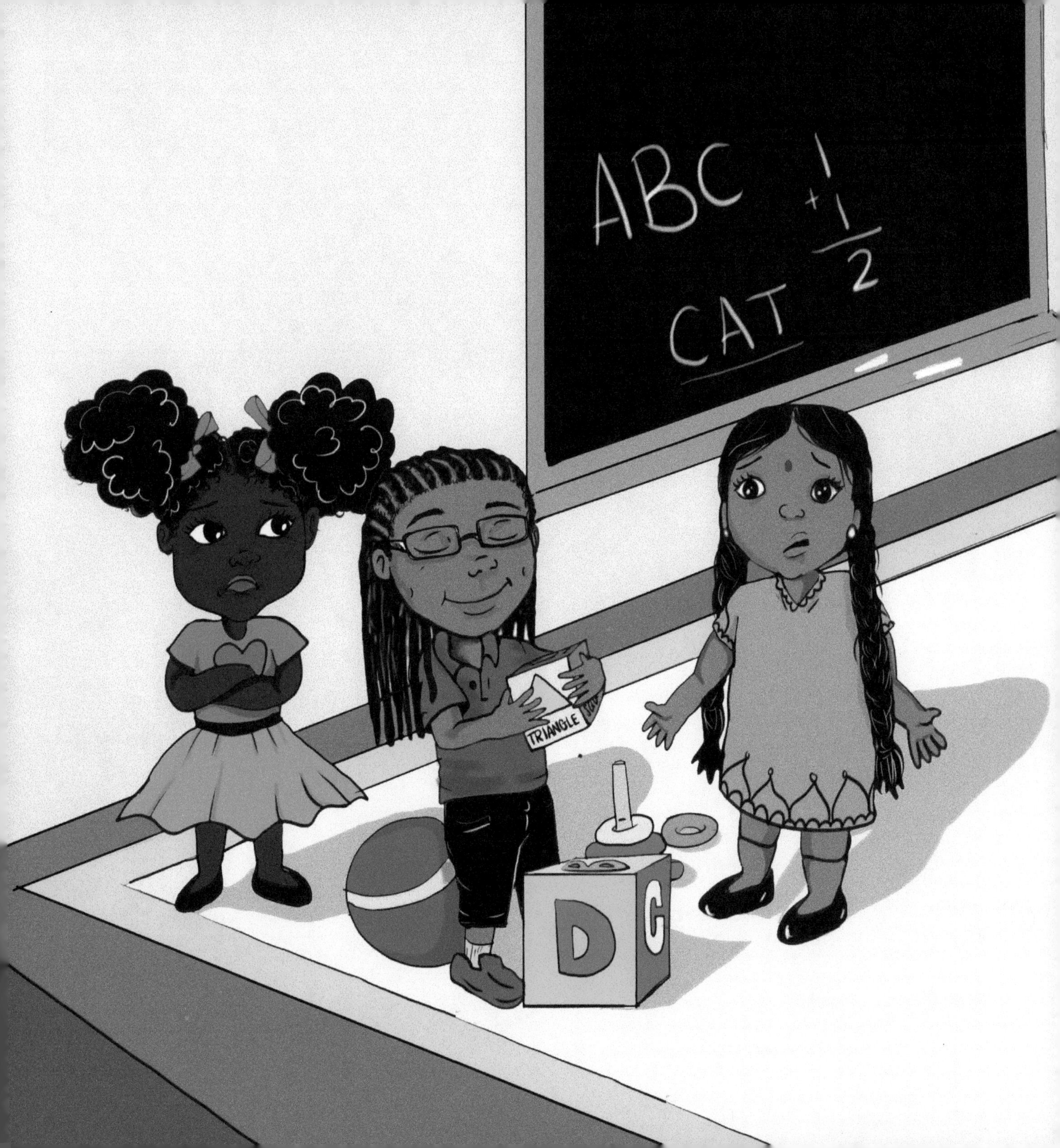
ABC
CAT
1
+1
2
TRIANGLE
D
C

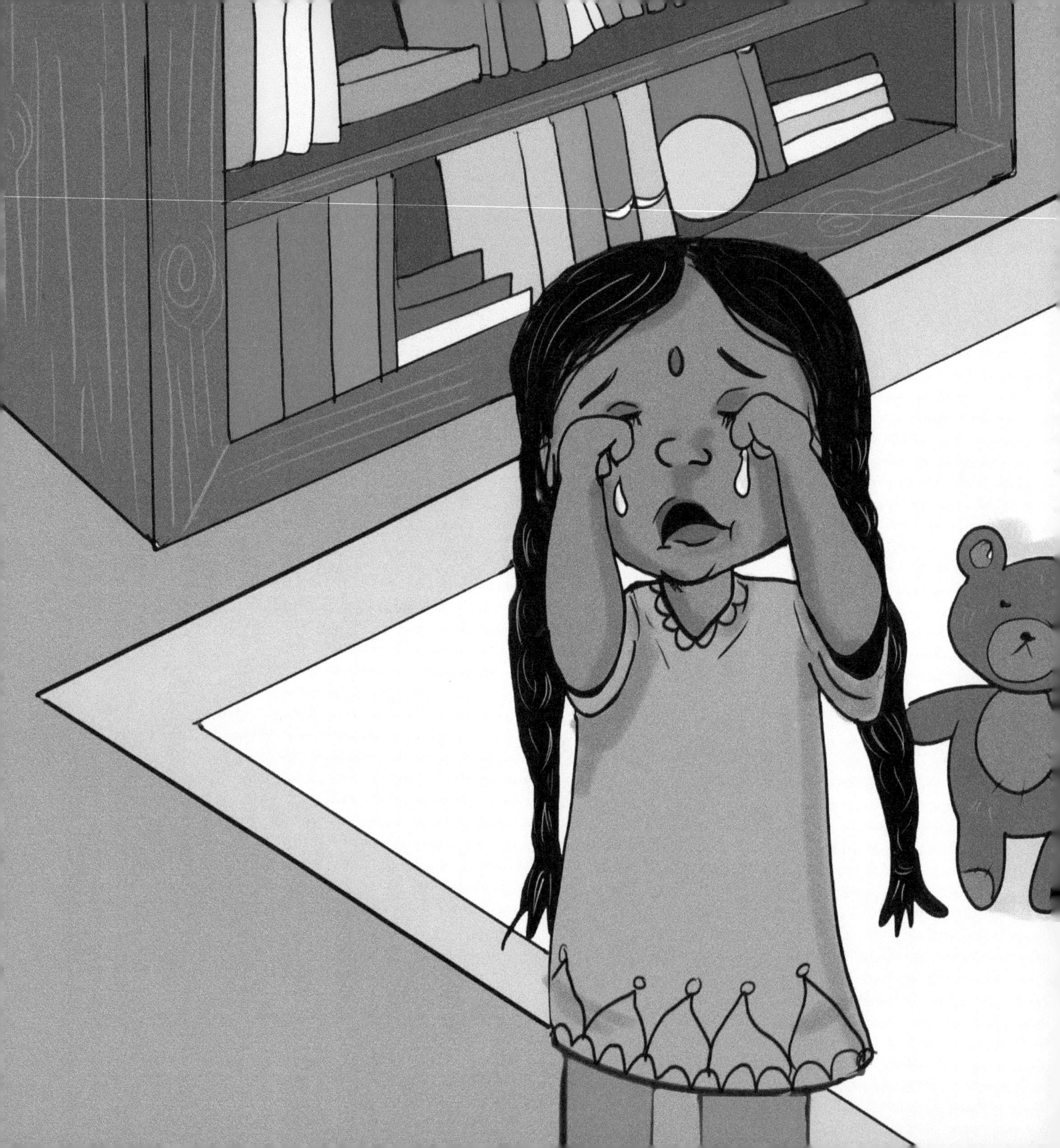

"No! These are for ME," Robert yelled as he snatched his blocks away.

Janaiya walked away and was upset. She started crying because her feelings were hurt.

"THERE GOES EL'REY," all of the kids pointed out.

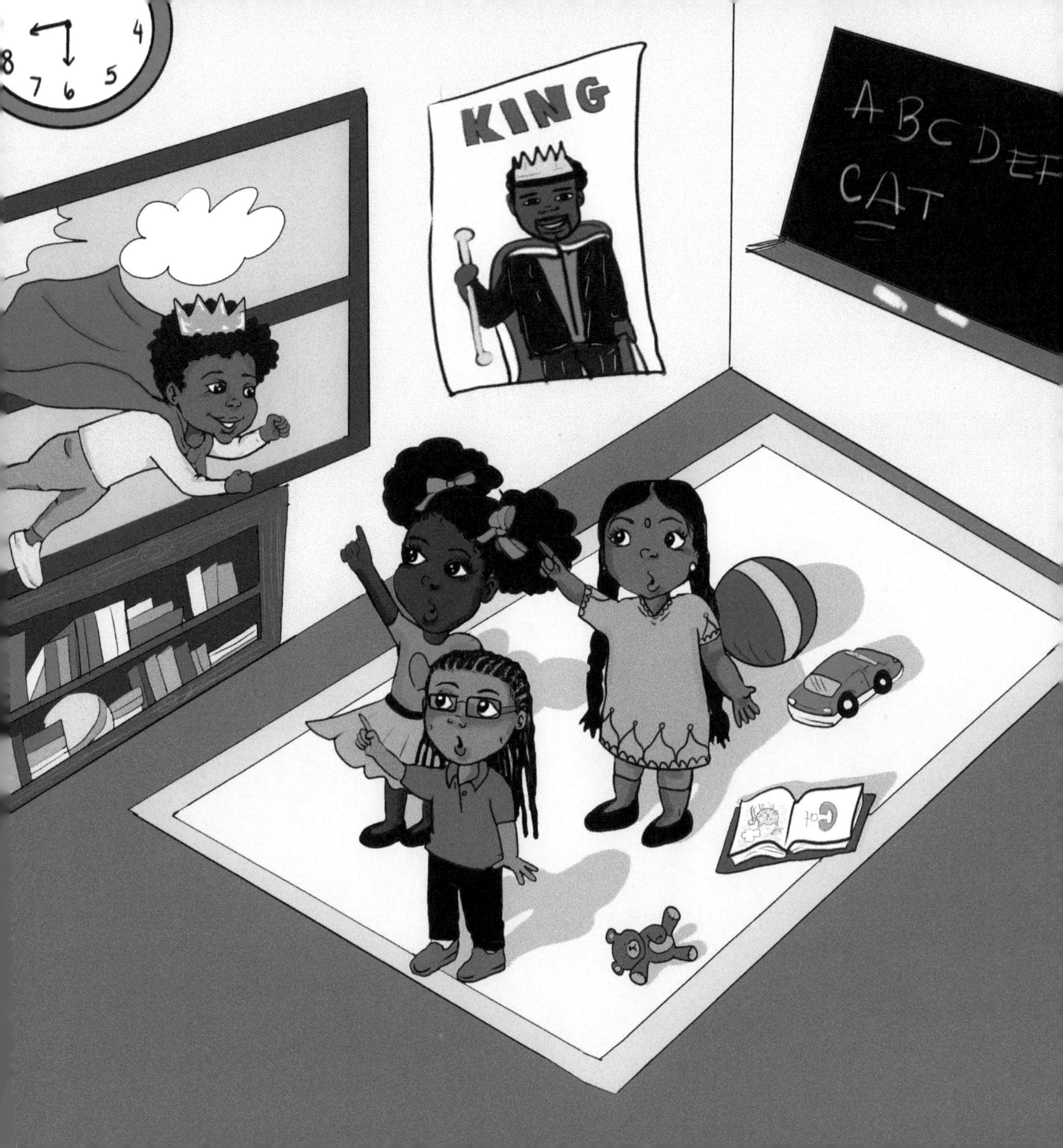
KING
ABCDEF
CAT

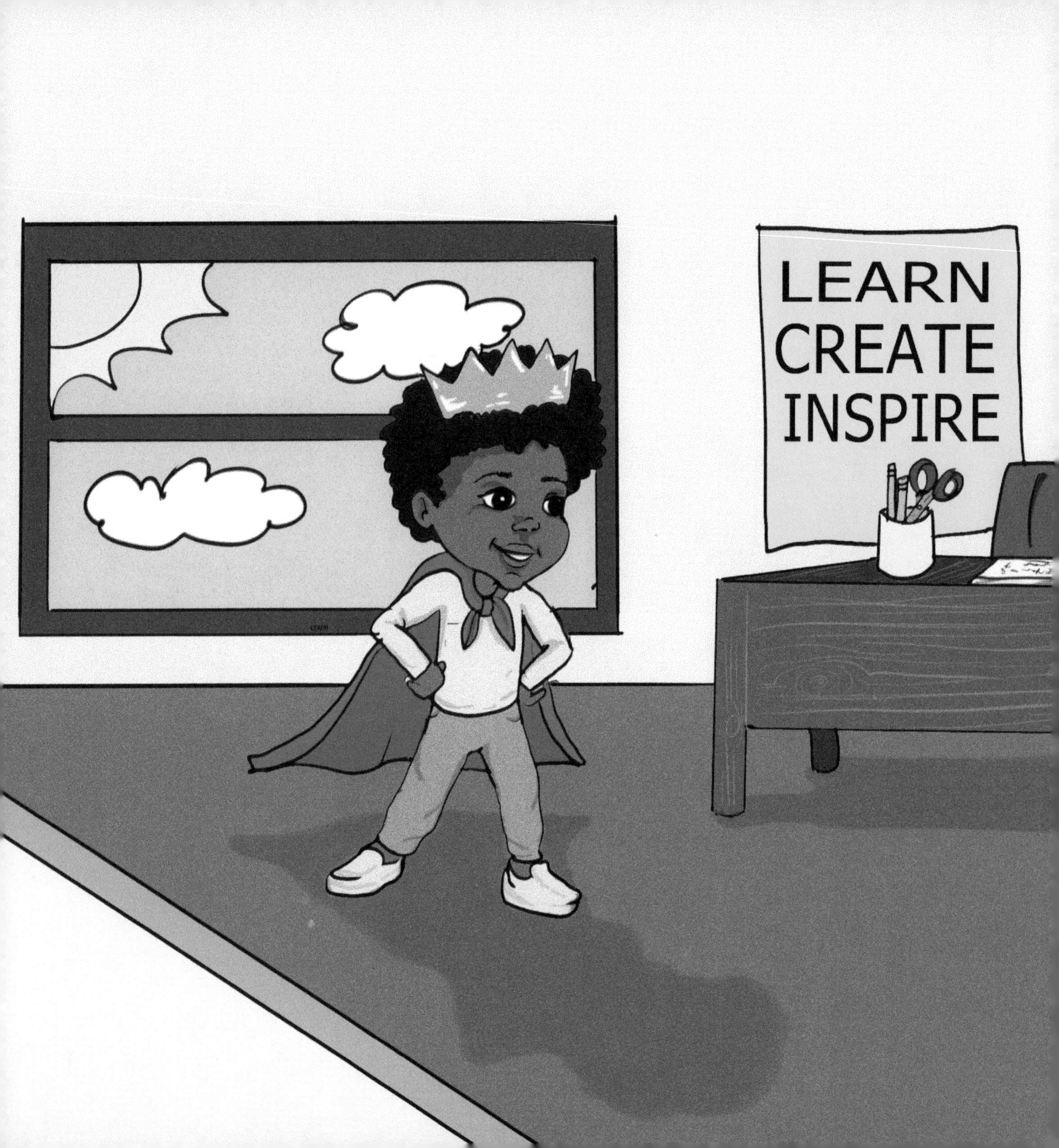
LEARN
CREATE
INSPIRE

"The King is here to solve this Problem!
Why won't you guys share your blocks?" The king asked.

"Because they're mine!" Tasha replied.

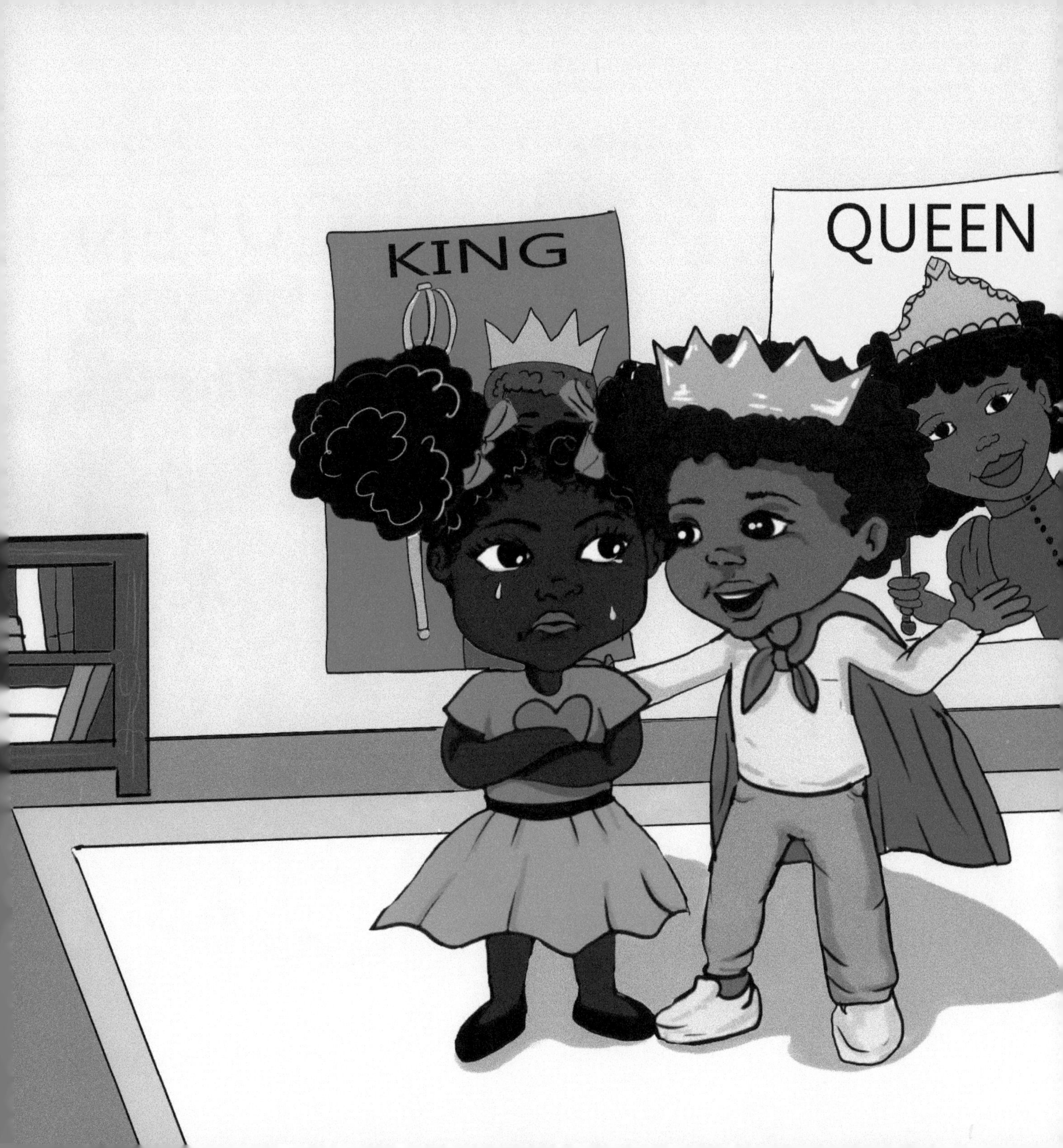
KING
QUEEN

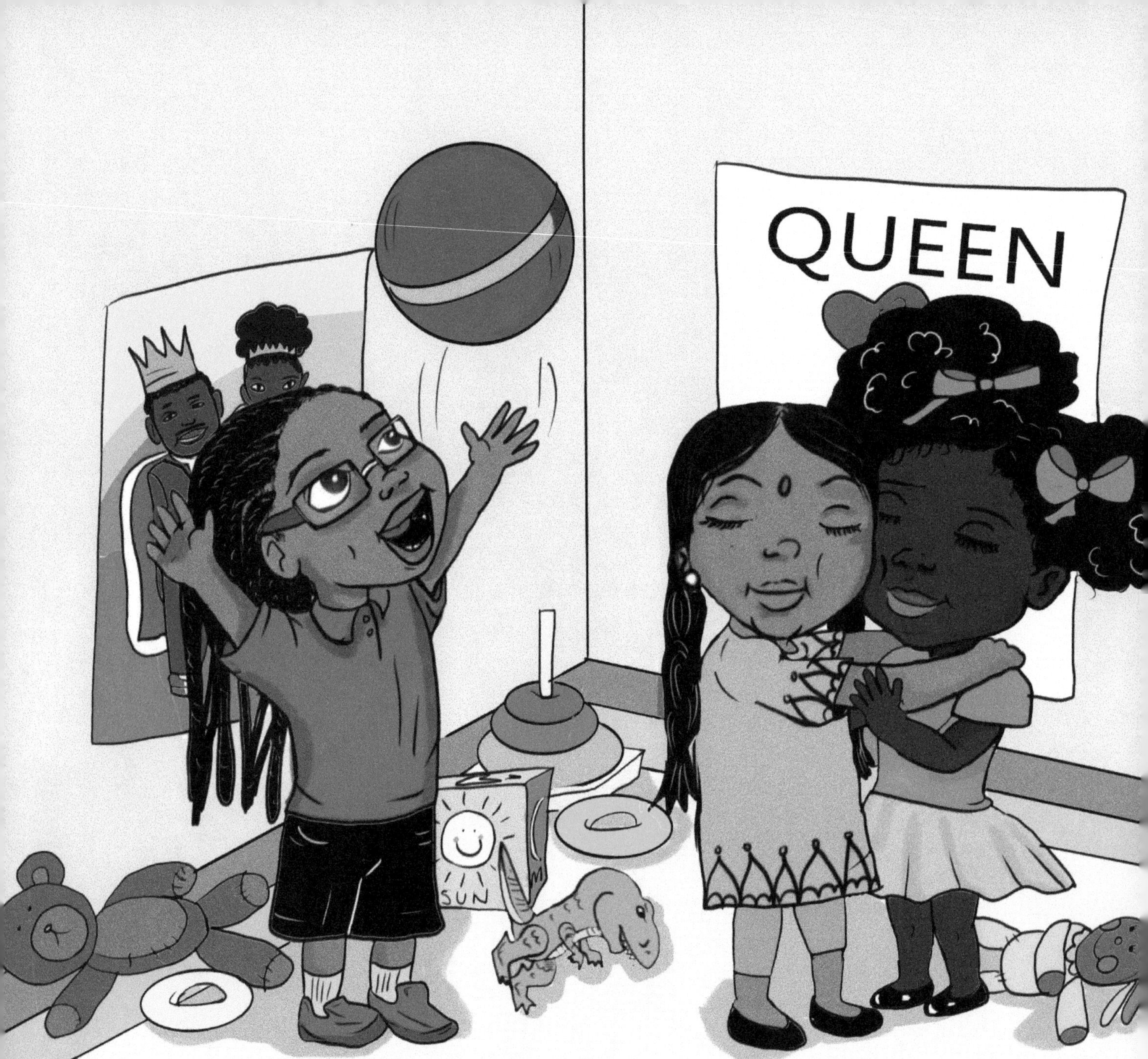
QUEEN
SUN

"You guys have more than enough blocks to share. It is important that we are nice to our friends and share with others. We don't want to see our friends upset." The king told the class.

Then all of the children gave Janaiya their toys and blocks. Everyone gave her a big hug and she smiled.

"OUT GOES THE KING!!!
Another problem Solved with EL'REY"!

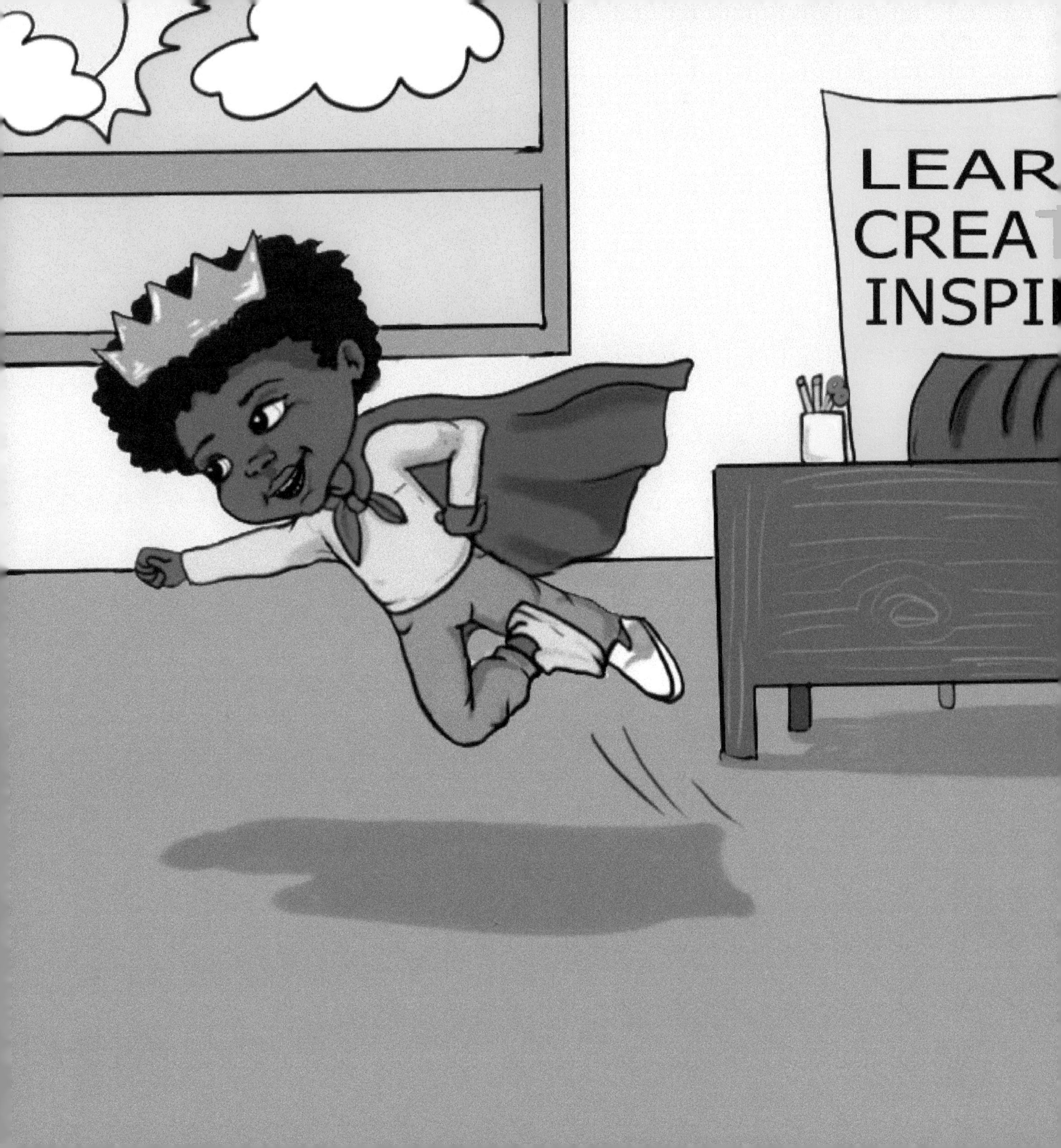
LEAR
CREA
INSPI

CPSIA information can be obtained
at www.ICGtesting.com
Printed in the USA
BVHW022137130321
602168BV00001B/3

9 781970 079753